The Baby's Book of
BABIES

by Kathy Henderson
Photographs by Anthea Sieveking

The Baby's Book of
BABIES

A Puffin Pied Piper

Where are the babies?
Turn the pages
and you'll find them
everywhere...

squeaking, peeping,
crawling, creeping,

jumping, flying,
riding high,

babies rolling,
looking, strolling,

stopping, flopping,
squashing the shopping,

babies tasting,
chewing, pasting,

sticky fingers here and there,

bathing, splashing,
laughing, catching

soapy bubbles in the air,

lazing, dozy,
snoozing, cozy,
lying down
or in the chair,

round ones, long ones,
small ones, strong ones,
babies, babies
everywhere!

PUFFIN PIED PIPER BOOKS
Published by the Penguin Group
Penguin Books USA Inc., 375 Hudson Street, New York, New York 10014, U.S.A.
Penguin Books Ltd, 27 Wrights Lane, London W8 5TZ, England
Penguin Books Australia Ltd, Ringwood, Victoria, Australia
Penguin Books Canada Ltd, 10 Alcorn Avenue, Toronto, Ontario, Canada M4V 3B2
Penguin Books (N.Z.) Ltd, 182–190 Wairau Road, Auckland 10, New Zealand
Penguin Books Ltd, Registered Offices: Harmondsworth, Middlesex, England

First published in hardcover in the United States 1989 by
Dial Books for Young Readers
A Division of Penguin Books USA Inc.

Published in Great Britain by Frances Lincoln • Windward
Concept copyright © 1988 by Frances Lincoln
Text copyright © 1988 by Kathy Henderson
Photographs copyright © 1988 by Anthea Sieveking
All rights reserved
Library of Congress Catalog Card Number: 88-20428
Printed in Hong Kong
First Puffin Pied Piper Printing 1993
ISBN 0-14-054882-3
A Pied Piper Book is a registered trademark of
Dial Books for Young Readers, a division of Penguin Books USA Inc.,
® TM 1,163,686 and ® TM 1,054,312.
3 5 7 9 10 8 6 4

THE BABY'S BOOK OF BABIES
is also available in hardcover from
Dial Books for Young Readers.

The publishers would like to thank
all the babies and parents
who took part in this book.

About the Author and Photographer

Kathy Henderson has written several books for children, including *15 Ways to Go to Bed,* a book about the games children—and parents—play when it's time to go to bed. She has also written stories and poems for children's radio programs in Great Britain. Much of her work is inspired by her three children, who are a constant source of ideas—and surprises.

After receiving training in photography at the Oxford School of Art, **Anthea Sieveking** set up a studio, and began photographing such famous people as Sir Winston Churchill. After having two babies, she became interested in photographing children, specializing in pregnancy and childbirth. Now a renowned photographer, her photographs have appeared in many books, including *What's Inside?, What Color?,* and *How Many?,* all published by Dial.